For my best friend, Louise
- J. L.

tiger tales
5 River Road, Suite 128, Wilton, CT 06897
Published in the United States 2017
Originally published in Great Britain 2017
by Little Tiger Press

ISBN-13: 978-1-68010-065-5
ISBN-10: 1-68010-065-3
Printed in China
LTP/1400/1822/0217

10 9 8 7 6 5 4 3 2 1

For more insight and activities,
visit us at www.tigertalesbooks.com

The Only Lonely PANDA

by Jonny Lambert

Deep in the dewy forest,
where flamingos danced
and butterflies fluttered,
Panda sat alone.

"I wish I had a friend," he sighed.

Then Panda saw her.
"Wow . . . **look!** Maybe she
will be my friend."

But Panda didn't know
how to make friends.
I wonder what the other animals do,
he thought.

Graceful flamingos make friends by dancing together.

"That's it!" Panda exclaimed. "I will dance . . .

". . . like a feathery flamingo.

Then the panda will be my friend.

“How could anything

possibly

go . . .

"... wrong.

Oof!"

Panda picked himself up and watched playful lemurs make friends by bouncing together.

"Perfect!" Panda announced. "I will bounce instead . . .

". . . like a leaping lemur.

Then the panda will
definitely want to be my friend.

"Whee!

Watch me fly!

Woo-hoo!

"Oomph!"

Down on the ground, Panda spotted two blue-footed boobies.

"Aha!" he cried. "I will **stomp** and **strut** like a booby, then we will be friends.

“Now, where did she go?”
But Panda hadn’t looked very far before . . .

. . . he spotted a handsome peacock.

"Feathers!" Panda exclaimed.

"If I had a dazzling tail of feathers, she'd surely be my friend.

All I need is one or two . . .

“Yikes!

I’m sorry!”

"Phew!" Panda puffed.
"Who needs fancy feathers anyway?"
Panda picked up some bamboo and
wiggled his bottom.

"This tail wiggle just **has** to work!" he said.

"Here we go . . .

"Rats."

Panda sighed.
"She will *never*, *ever* be my friend."
And he trudged off to eat his dinner.

Deep in the dewy forest,
where lemurs leaped
and peacocks pranced,
Panda sat eating alone . . .

. . . but not for long.

“Hello!” said the other panda.
“That looks tasty.”

“It’s delicious!” nodded Panda,
and then he had his best idea yet.
“Would you like to share?”

And so they did.

Among the lush leaves,
two pandas ate and played together . . .
and became the best of friends.